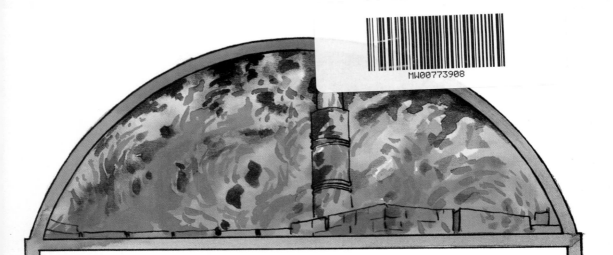

The ArtScroll Children's Holiday Series

Yaffa Ganz

TISHAH B'AV
THE FOUR FASTS
WITH BINA, BENNY AND CHAGGAI HAYONAH

Illustrated by Liat Benyaminy Ariel

HALOM! I'm Chaggai Hayonah, Chaggai the Holiday Dove. Bina and Benny and I are getting ready for Tishah B'Av, the ninth day of the month of Av.

"Did you find your sneakers, Benny?"

"Yep. They were under the bed, just as I thought."

"It's so funny, fasting and not wearing leather shoes on a regular day."

"It's not funny at all! It's very sad. And it's not a regular day either. Tishah B'Av is the day the *Beis Hamikdash* was destroyed! Oof!" Benny found another knot in his shoelace.

"I didn't mean funny-for-laughing!" said Bina. "I meant it's strange. No other day is quite like Tishah B'Av. It's not a regular day, but it's not a holiday either. It's a sad day for us now, but one day, it will be a very happy day for *Am Yisrael*."

☙ ☙ ☙

Bina is right. Someday Tishah B'Av will be a day of rejoicing for the Jewish people. But until then, the ninth of Av is one of four fast days when we mourn the *Churban* –– the destruction of Jerusalem and the *Beis Hamikdash*.

These four days are:

The Fast of the Fourth Month: SHIVAH ASAR B'TAMMUZ
   (seventeenth of Tammuz)
The Fast of the Fifth Month: TISHAH B'AV (ninth of Av)
The Fast of the Seventh Month: TZOM GEDALYAH
   (Fast of Gedalyah — third of Tishrei)
The Fast of the Tenth Month: ASARAH B'TEVES
   (tenth of Teves)

"Why do we need *four* fast days?" asked Benny. "Isn't one enough?"

"Oh, no!" said Chaggai. "Not when so many terrible things happened, each on a different day! Shall I tell you about it?" Bina and Benny sat back to listen.

t the very very beginning of things, even before He created the world, G-d created the Torah. Then He created everything else, so that one day, the Jewish people would accept the Torah and fill the world with holiness.

But in order to keep all the laws of the Torah, the Jewish people must live in *Eretz Yisrael,* the Land of Israel. *Hashem* had prepared the Land of Canaan for this purpose. It was a very special place — a good land, a pleasant land, a Holy Land, a land flowing with milk and honey. Of all the lands in the world, this is the one perfect place for G-d's people to keep G-d's Torah.

Eretz Yisrael is not like any other land. All year long, from beginning to end, G-d Himself watches and cares for this Land. It is a holy Land, and in order to live there, the Jews must be a holy people. Then we will live in peace and plenty. Our vineyards will be full of grapes, our fields full of wheat, our orchards full of fruit. But if we do not keep the laws of the Torah, the rains will not fall, the crops will not grow, sickness and war and bad times will come. And the Jewish people will be sent away from the Land until they return to *Hashem* and His Torah.

But even then, even when we are not in the Land of Israel, the Land is still ours. G-d promised Avraham *Avinu*:

> And I shall give you and your children after you . . . the entire Land of Canaan, to keep forever. . . You shall live in this land and I will be with you and I shall bless you . . .

We are the children of Avraham, and the Land belongs to us forever and ever. One day, just as G-d promised, all the Jews in the world shall return home.

"I'm going to *Eretz Yisrael* just as soon as I can!" announced Benny. "I just have to get a little older first!"

They shall make Me a Holy
Temple and I shall dwell
within them.

(*Shemos* 25:8)

All of *Eretz Yisrael* is holy, but Jerusalem is the holiest place of all. And the *Beis Hamikdash*, the Temple, is the holiest part of Jerusalem. It is *Hashem's* "house" — His *bayis* — where the *Kohanim* brought the *korbanos* and the *Leviim* played their instruments and sang. It is where *Am Yisrael* came three times a year: Pesach, Shavuos, and Succos. It is where the people brought the *Korban Pesach* and the *Bikkurim* and where they watched the *Simchas Beis Hashoeyvah*. It is where all the people came to sacrifice and pray and learn Torah and rejoice.

The *Beis Hamikdash* was the center of the world. Even the non-Jews knew that this was the place where the G-d of Israel blessed all the nations of the world.

❀ ❀ ❀

How beautiful the Temple was with its stone walls and golden doors and heavy gates! The people gathered outside in the great open courtyards. Inside the *Heichal,* with its huge cedar beams and its towering ceiling, were the wonderful golden Menorah, the golden Table, and the golden Altar. And inside the *Kodesh Hakodashim* —

the Holy of Holies — was the *Aron Hakodesh*, the Holy Ark which contained the Tablets of Stone, the flask of *mahn*, Aaron's staff and the original *Sefer Torah* written by Moshe *Rabbeinu*.

The Western Light on the golden Menorah was always lit; twelve breads were always on the golden Table; and the fragrant smell of the *ketores* on the golden Altar always filled the air. And the *Shechinah* — the Presence of G-d — always hovered above the Temple.

our hundred and eighty years before the *Beis Hamikdash* was built, the Jews received the Torah at Sinai and began their journey to the Land of Israel. But the closer they came to the Land, the more they worried. What was the Land really like? Would they be happy there? Would they have to fight hard to capture it? Would they win? The people were worried and afraid.

G-d gave Moshe permission to send out scouts to tour the Land. They were told to bring back some of its fruit. Twelve noble and important men were chosen, one from each tribe. For forty days they toured the country. On the eighth of Av, they returned, carrying huge grapes,

pomegranates and dates. But they also brought back frightening news.

"The Land is truly a land flowing with milk and honey," said ten of the scouts. "Just look at the size of this fruit! But the cities are strong, their walls are thick, and the people are giants, just like the fruit! We will *never* be able to capture this Land!" Only two of the scouts, Yehoshua Bin Nun and Calev Ben Yefuneh, disagreed. "Let us go up to the Land," they insisted. "We *will* capture it and live in it, just as G-d promised!"

But the people wouldn't listen to Yehoshua and Calev. That night, the ninth of Av, they cried and complained. "Let us go back to Egypt," they shouted at Moshe. "What good is it if we are killed in the Land?!"

Hashem was angry. "They saw My miracles but they do not believe in Me! Do they complain of My goodly Land? Then they shall not enter it! They shall wander in the desert for forty years until they die. Their children shall enter the Land without them. Because they cried and shed tears for no reason today, this shall become a day of sorrow and tears throughout the generations!"

On this very same day — the ninth of Av — almost 1000 years later, the first *Beis Hamikdash* was destroyed. And on the ninth of Av, almost 500 years after the first *Churban*, the Second Temple was also destroyed.

avid *Hamelech* had drawn the plans and made many of the preparations for building the *Beis Hamikdash*. His son Shlomo built the House. For seven busy years, the work continued. The entire nation helped. Finally, in the Hebrew year 2928, the *Beis Hamikdash* was ready. Shlomo made a great celebration as the first sacrifices were brought. How happy everyone was! How holy the people were!

At first, all was well. But slowly, many of the Jews began to forget the laws of the Torah. They began to worship idols. Some of them stole or lied or killed. These people no longer acted like a holy nation, so they were no longer worthy of living in the Land of Israel and having a *Beis Hamikdash*. G-d sent Nevuchadnezzar, the mighty and evil king of Bavel, to destroy the Temple.

Nevuchadnezzar captured the countryside and surrounded the city. He broke through the walls and attacked the Temple. But *Hashem* did not allow the Babylonians to set His House afire. Instead, He sent four angels to light the terrible flames. The House of G-d could only be conquered when G-d had removed the *Shechinah* — His Holy Presence — from between its walls!

When the *Kohanim* saw that all was lost, they went up to the roof of the building. "*Hashem*!" they cried. "If we are no longer worthy of being the guardians of Your Temple, we are returning the keys to You!" And they threw the keys up to the sky.

A hand came out of the Heavens and took the keys, and the *Kohanim* jumped into the fire and died. Tens of thousands of Jews were killed in the war. Tens of thousands more were taken prisoner to Bavel. The roads were full of Jewish men, women and children in chains.

Hashem had destroyed His Holy House. He had poured His anger onto a building of wood and stone. But His people, the Jewish people, were not destroyed. They lived on. One day, they would return home and rebuild the Temple. Nevuchadnezzar and his army took all the gold and silver they could find, but they could not find the Holy Ark. That was hidden. It will be found when the Third *Beis Hamikdash* is built.

he Jews were in exile in Bavel for seventy years. On the seventieth year, many of the Jews returned to the Land of Israel. A large number of Jews had become very wealthy in Bavel. They wanted to stay in their comfortable houses. But the poorer people came with Zerubavel to build the House of G-d. At first, this *Bayis* was small and simple, but as time went on, they made it bigger and lovelier until it was the most beautiful building in the world.

This time, the Jews learned Torah and kept most of the *mitzvos,* but not all of them. They were very strict with some *mitzvos,* but not with others. Some of them argued and fought and did not respect or live peacefully with each other. Some made fun of the scholars. Some were not always kind and merciful and forgiving.

During the time of the Second Temple, the powerful

Roman Empire arose and ruled the world. When Rome sent its armies to Israel to conquer the Land, the Jews revolted. The Jews were good soldiers, and for many years, they fought the Romans. Yet even then, they continued to fight with each other too.

Finally, Rome decided to put an end to the troublesome Jews. For three long years, the Roman armies beseiged the city of Jerusalem. Then, on the ninth of Av, the Roman general Titus entered the *Beis Hamikdash* and burnt it down. The Romans plowed up the land in the city and poured salt into the ground so that nothing could grow there. Only the *Kosel Hamaaravi,* the Western Wall of the Temple Mount, was left standing.

One of the great teachers and scholars, Rabbi Yochanan ben Zakkai, had escaped from the city. He surrendered to the Romans and persuaded them to permit the *chachamim* in the town of Yavneh to continue teaching Torah. The school there became a great *yeshivah* and even though the *Beis Hamikdash* was destroyed and most of the Jews were sent away from the Land of Israel, the Jewish people and the Torah continued to exist. Today, there is no more Roman Empire, nor are there any Romans. But *Am Yisrael* and the Torah are still here.

"But you still haven't told us why we have *four* fast days instead of one," said Benny.

"That's because I haven't finished yet," said the dove. "But I'll tell you right now. . ."

he Fast of the Tenth Month is Asarah B'Teves. On the tenth of Teves, Nevuchadnezzar of Bavel laid seige to the city of Jerusalem. His armies surrounded the city. No one could enter or leave; no supplies could be brought in. The people in Jerusalem began to starve. Nevuchadnezzar was sure he could conquer the city quickly, but the siege lasted three long years. Hashem wanted to give the Jews a chance to do *teshuvah* and save the *Beis Hamikdash* from destruction, but they didn't. So Asarah B'Teves was the beginning of the *churban*, and the Prophets declared it a day of fasting.

"What good is fasting?" asked Benny. "Fasting won't rebuild the *Beis Hamikdash,* will it?"

"No it won't, but it might help *us* remember to do *teshuvah* and be the kind of Jews *Hashem* wants us to be! And as soon as we do that, *Hashem* will arrange things top speed so that the *Beis Hamikdash* is rebuilt!"

he second of the four fast days is the Fast of the Fourth Month — Shivah Asar B'Tammuz. Several important things happened on this day, the seventeenth of Tammuz.

After the people received the Torah at Sinai, Moshe *Rabbeinu* went back up the mountain for forty days. But the people made a mistake. They thought Moshe would return on the sixteenth of Tammuz. When he didn't come back, they were sure he had died on the mountain. They were very frightened. They begged Aharon to give them a new leader, a new god. Aharon knew that Moshe would soon return and he tried to make them wait, but they wouldn't listen.

Moshe came down on the seventeenth of Tammuz, which was the fortieth day, just as he had promised. He was carrying the *Luchos Habris* — the two stone tablets with the Ten Commandments. When he found the people dancing around a Golden Calf, he was so angry

that he threw the *Luchos* down and they broke into many pieces. It was a sad and terrible day for *Am Yisrael*.

But that's not all. Years later, in the time of the First *Beis Hamikdash*, Nevuchadnezzar broke through the walls of *Yerushalayim* on the seventeenth of Tammuz. The Prophets therefore decreed it a fast day to remember this terrible event. Then, in the time of the Second *Beis Hamikdash*, Titus also broke through the walls of the city on the seventeenth of Tammuz.

ishah B'Av is the Fast of the Fifth Month. On the ninth day of the month of Av, both Temples were destroyed. The first *Beis Hamikdash* was destroyed by Nevuchadnezzar of Bavel on Tishah B'Av. The Second *Beis Hamikdash* was destroyed by Titus of Rome on Tishah B'Av four hundred ninety years later. The first one had stood for four hundred ten years, and the second one for four hundred twenty.

Tens of thousands of Jews were killed. Many others were sent away as slaves to Rome. For almost 2000 years, the Jewish nation wandered from country to country, never at home. They no longer ruled their

beloved Land; they no longer had their beloved *Beis Hamikdash*. Only the *Kosel Hamaaravi*, the Western Wall around *Har Habayis*, was still standing.

But we never forgot Jerusalem. Jews all over the world turn to face *Yerushalayim* when they pray. And those who could, have always traveled to the Land of Israel to pray at the *Kosel.* Today, millions of Jews are living in the Land of Israel.

We hope and pray that *Mashiach* will come soon and the Third *Beis Hamikdash* will be built. Then all of our people will return to *Eretz Yisrael* where we can be a true *mamleches kohanim v'goy kadosh* — a Kingdom of Priests and a Holy Nation.

Many other misfortunes and disasters took place on Tishah B'Av. In the year 1492, the Jews of Spain were given a terrible choice: Become Christians or leave the country by Tishah B'Av! Three hundred thousand Jews — old people and young, men, women, and little children — refused to convert. They chose to remain Jews. On Tishah B'Av day, the last group left Spain. All the roads and all the ports were crowded with Jews, clutching their children and their small bags of belongings, preparing to march or sail away. Their property and wealth was left behind.

Worst of all, many of them had no place to go. No country wanted them; no one offered them a real home. For years, many of them wandered far across lands and sea. Many fell sick and died. Others were killed or captured as slaves. It was a terrible time for the Jewish people, a true Tishah B'Av tragedy.

The last of the four fast days is Tzom Gedalyah — the Fast of Gedalyah. Tzom Gedalyah is on the third day in the month of Tishrei.

When Nevuchadnezzar destroyed the Temple and sent the Jews to Bavel, he didn't send everyone away. Some Jews still remained behind. Nevuchadnezzar appointed a Jewish governor — Gedalyah ben Achikam — to rule them. Gedalyah was a good and righteous man. The people loved him, and as long as he ruled, they lived in peace. Jews who had run away during the war returned. They planted vineyards and tilled the land and were happy. But then Gedalyah was killed. Nevuchadnezzar was angry and the Jews were afraid that he would take revenge. They ran away, leaving the country empty and in ruins.

We fast on Tzom Gedalyah because Gedalyah's death meant that no more Jews were left in the Land of Israel and thousands more Jews were killed. When a righteous man like Gedalyah dies, his death is like the destruction of the House of G-d.

our whole days to fast!" complained Benny. "What a lot of time not to eat!"

"It's not four entire days," said Chaggai. "On three of the days, we only fast during the daytime — from before sunrise until the stars come out at night. The only time we fast an entire day — almost twenty-five hours, just like on Yom Kippur — is Tishah B'Av. But don't worry, Benny. You're young. You don't have to fast yet!"

"We don't wash or use perfumes or wear leather shoes on Tishah B'Av either," said Bina. "Just like on Yom Kippur. Is there anything else we don't do, Chaggai?"

"Well, let me see. There are three weeks between Shivah Asar B'Tammuz and Tishah B'Av. During this time we don't cut our hair, buy new clothes, listen to music, get married or have parties. And during the nine days before Tishah B'Av, we don't take baths, go swimming, mend or sew, decorate our houses, or do any kind of celebrating.

"On Erev Tishah B'Av, we eat a full meal in the late afternoon. Then we sit down on the floor or on a low stool and eat again — the *Seudah Mafsekes.* This is a sad meal, only bread and water. Some people also eat hard eggs."

"Then we take off our regular, leather shoes and put on sneakers or slippers or other shoes which aren't made of leather and we go to *shul*!" said Bina.

"In our *shul* we turn the lights down," said Benny. "We

sit on the floor with candles while the *chazzan* reads *Eichah.* Yirmiyahu *Hanavi* wrote the Book of *Eichah.* He describes the destruction of the Temple and the suffering of the Jewish people."

"*Eichah* has such a sad tune," said Bina. "It makes me cry."

"Me, too," said Benny softly. "But remember what you said, Bina! Someday Tishah B'Av will be a happy day. Someday we'll have a new *Beis Hamikdash* and this time, it won't be destroyed!"

"Tishah B'Av is *Mashiach's* birthday," said Chaggai, "and once *Mashiach* arrives, the *Beis Hamikdash* can't be far behind!"

"We should remember the *Churban Beis Hamikdash* all year long," said Benny. "not just on Tishah B'Av."

"We do," said Chaggai.

"We do?"

"Yes, indeed. Just look around you."

Benny looked. "I don't see anything special," he said.

"I do!" said Bina. "The wall facing the door! Remember, Benny? Abba didn't paint there. He left an unpainted square so that our house wouldn't be perfect so long as *Hashem's* House is not standing."

"I forgot! But I remember something else. At Reuven's wedding, he broke the glass under the *chuppah*, so that even at a *simchah* like a wedding, something would remind us of *Yerushalayim.*"

"At some weddings," said Chaggai, "the groom even rubs ashes on his head, in the same spot as he places his *tefillin* every morning, as a sign of mourning for Yerushalayim and the *Beis Hamikdash*."

"I'm glad the bride doesn't have to do that!" said Bina. "But Imma told me there is a custom for the bride not to wear all of her jewelry under the *chuppah* so that she won't be all splendid and elegant when the *Beis Hamikdash* is still in ruins."

"And I learned that the first time we see the *Kosel*, we tear our jacket or shirt, just like a mourner does when someone in the family has died."

"And if we keep remembering to do all of these things," said Chaggai, "we shall surely see Jerusalem and the *Beis Hamikdash* rebuilt in all of their splendor and glory! *Chazal* told us that. . .

Whoever mourns the destruction of Jerusalem will surely rejoice in its rebuilding!

Someday soon, the long exile will end. *Mashiach*, a descendant of the family of David, will reign as King of the Jewish people. The Jews from all four corners of the world will return home to the Land of Israel. A new *Beis Hamikdash* will be built, never to be destroyed again. And there will be peace in the world, no more fighting, no more war.

All the nations will finally understand that *Hashem* is King of the World, that He is One, and that *Am Yisrael* is His people. And when that happens . . .

> The Fast of the Fourth Month, and the Fast of the Fifth, and the Fast of the Seventh, and the Fast of the Tenth shall become times of joy and gladness and cheerful feasts for the House of Yehudah. . .
>
> (*Zecharyah* 8:19)

"And then," said Benny, "instead of fasting and being sad, we can eat and be happy!"

"And instead of living here, we will live on our own land in *Eretz Yisrael*!" said Bina.

"And instead of dreaming about the *Beis Hamikdash*, we will go there and see it!" said Benny again.

"Just remember," said Chaggai with a smile, "everyone else will be going there too. It might get crowded."

"No, it won't!" said Bina and Benny together. "In the courtyards of the *Beis Hamikdash*, there will always be enough room for *all* of *Am Yisrael*!"

אָמֵן, כֵּן יְהִי רָצוֹן.
Amen, so may it be.

GLOSSARY

Am Yisrael — the People of Israel

baruch Hashem — Thank G-d; Blessed be G-d

Bavel — Babylonia

Beis Hamikdash — The Holy Temple in Jerusalem

Bikkurim — the First Fruits

chachamim — sages

Chazal — the Sages of the Talmud

chazzan — a cantor

chuppah — the wedding canopy

Churban — the Destruction of the Temple

Eichah — the scroll of *Eichah* [Lamentations]

Eretz Yisrael — the Land of Israel

esrog — the citron fruit used in the holiday of Succos

galus — exile

Heichal — the Temple building

Hashem — G-d

ketores — the incense offered in the Temple

Kohanim — priests

korban/korbanos — offerings and sacrifices in the Temple

Leviim — the tribe of Levi; they served as assistants to the priests in the Temple

lulav — palm leaves

mahn — the manna the Jews ate in the desert

Mashiach — the Messiah

Moshe Rabbeinu — Moses our teacher

Sefer Torah — a Torah scroll

Shlomo — King Solomon, son of King David

shul (Yiddish) — synagogue

yeshivah — a school of Torah study

Yirmiyahu Hanavi — the prophet Jeremiah